SOLSTICE GIFTS

A WINDBORNE HOLIDAY SHORT STORY

Books by Laurel Wanrow

The Windborne Series ~ *for young adults*
The Witch of the Meadows
Guardian of the Pines
Lost Whisperer of the Seas
Keepers of the Sea Cliffs
Solstice Gifts (Holiday Short Story)

The Luminated Threads Series ~ *for ages 15 & up*
The Unraveling, Volume One
The Twisting, Volume Two
The Binding, Volume Three
The Luminated Threads Volumes 1-3 Box Set

Science Fiction Romance ~ *for adults*
Passages

SOLSTICE GIFTS

A WINDBORNE HOLIDAY SHORT STORY

LAUREL WANROW

Sprouting Star Press

Copy Edit by Joyce Lamb
Cover Design by J. Kathleen Cheney
Created with Vellum

Wanrow, Laurel
Solstice Gifts / Laurel Wanrow. ~ 1st ed.
ISBN 978-1-943469-18-5
First Edition: November 2019

For Clarissa: Your enthusiasm for Fern and Beri's story has spurred me on!

1

VACATIONS ARE FOR...

In the Rocky Mountains of Colorado

Beri of the Moors decided the best course of action—for him, at any rate—was to stand back this Solstice and take direction when given. And to keep his thoughts on human holiday celebrations to himself. Beside him, Fern Fields nearly skipped up the gravel road with a lively energy equaling that of the fox he'd spotted chasing a hare last week. Everyone riding the school bus up the canyon had enthusiastically talked about their holiday plans, but of course he and Fern couldn't say much about theirs, since their relatives would be arriving through a magical portal, not by car or plane.

"You are gonna love winter break," Fern gushed, and he had to smile. "What are you most excited about doing for your first Christmas?"

"Spending time with you," Beri said. "And sleeping."

Fern grinned, her brown eyes brightening. "Don't let my mom hear you say those two things in the same sentence." She swatted his chest, her hand sliding over his down vest to corral him around the neck. She pressed her lips to his.

Mmm, nice. Before he could draw her closer, she shifted back and laughed, her breath puffing white and warm in the chill mountain air.

"But I know what you mean," she said. "We never have enough time together." Long, black hair swinging, she linked her arm through his and tugged him along, clearly too impatient to kiss more.

Being an exchange student at Fern's human school ate up more hours than he'd expected when they first started dating, and because he still lived on the Isle of Giuthas, wizards there continued to request his help for various wildlife and magical tasks. Beri leaned toward Fern and whispered, "I dinnae tell the elders we had a break. I still plan to come here every day and nap on your couch."

"Ha. You wish!"

They turned onto another of the small mountain town's roads, and the roof of Fern and her mother's home came into view, the modern cabin hidden by evergreen boughs of Ponderosa pine and spruce trees.

"Do you think it'll snow today?" he asked. The one early snowfall in these mountains had melted fast with the warm weather that had followed. Compared to the coast of the British Isles where he'd grown up, Colorado's dry weather gave him no clue if another snowstorm was coming.

Fern glanced toward the clouds building in the afternoon skies. "It might. We should carry some ornament boxes from the garage as we head inside. One less trip for later."

Snow didn't hold the same interest for Colorado-reared Fern. "I can carry quite a lot," he said.

"We have a gazillion things Mom has made over the years. Glass pieces I wouldn't let her sell because I loved them so. Things I made that she saved and ones we've traded for at craft shows. You'll love the animals! It's mostly animals. There's this

sweet little hedgehog made of a dried teasel with a red scarf..."
And she was off, describing one animal after another.

'Twas odd to hear her coo over wild beasts wearing bells and
whatnot. From the talk of other students in his classes, gift-
giving was a big part of their human holiday. He'd quizzed Fern
on the traditions that she and her mum, Lady Heather, kept and
was relieved to learn they more so celebrated Winter Solstice,
like the Windborne wizards he'd grown up with, and in a
modest fashion. Good, because no one on the isle had the trade
credit in the human world to do anything extravagant, least of
all him, an apprentice.

Still, he worried that the gift he'd prepared for Fern might
not be enough. It'd be the first thing he gave her. Courting—or
rather, dating—in the human world confused him, perhaps more
than attending one of their schools. There, his Scottish accent
and mannerisms allowed him to brush off the bits and bobs he
didn't understand. With Fern, he wanted to get things right.

She poked him. "So? What do you think? Will celebrating
Winter Solstice with us be as good as an Isle of Giuthas celebration?"

"It's more important that your mum and Merlin agreed we
should hold it at your cabin. They can find so much to fight
about." Fern's parents had been separated and out of contact
since she was two. Merlin, her father, had raised Beri after his
parents died, with Fern's brother, on the Isle of Giuthas where
they still lived—but the portal between the isle and the Fields'
cabin now got a lot of use.

"No kidding." Fern became quiet as they neared her home.
"Beneath it all, I think Mom appreciates how much Dad has
helped these last few months. The craziness of completing her
orders and selling at fall craft shows is over, and she's even
promised to quit glassworking early today. I'm gonna make her
stick to it, whether or not she thinks she has enough pieces for

tomorrow's show. Come on." Fern dragged him the last few yards to the garage that her mother used as a studio.

The door was locked and the window shades down. Fern keyed in the code.

"No, no, no!" came a muffled cry from inside. A moment later, Lady Heather cracked open the door, blocking its entrance, and they tumbled back.

A passerby would find that funny since Fern—six feet tall—and Beri—nearly six and a half—towered over Heather Fields' slight five feet of height. That extra height didn't matter, though. Lady Heather exuded energy, all the more to humans who had no idea what power it was. People deferred to the petite woman, even when she was dressed in a burn-stained sweatshirt over old jeans and her long hair was braided and tied back to keep it from her flameworking torch.

Brow furrowed, she looked between them. "What are you doing home from school?" she asked in her Irish accent.

"Half day, Mom," Fern said cheerily. "They know it's a waste to keep us there with vacation. Whatcha making? Secret holiday gifts?"

"Not so much secret as late. I have nae cooked in so long that I forgot how much time it would take."

Fern sniffed. "Bread," she said longingly. "You made bread. But why do you have the bread machine out here?"

Heather cocked her head. "Because your father has taken over my kitchen, and I remember quite well that his *taste* of a fresh loaf will leave us with little for our company."

"Not company, Mom. Family."

Lady Heather nodded, and a look passed between her and Fern before they both glanced Beri's way. This had something to do with Fern's unusual mood, but he had no idea what. He'd known Fern for four months, but her moods remained a mystery. Like why she acted like a skittery hare this afternoon. Being off of school? The gifts? The special treats they'd be having for the Solstice celebration? He could ask, but sometimes Fern didn't seem to know herself. He just had to hope he knew her well enough to have picked a gift she'd like.

"Er, aye," he said. "I have been Merlin and Raven's family for so long, I promise I've forgotten how to be company. Can I help with something?"

Lady Heather sighed, and Fern looked amused as she poked him. "Just remember, we're *not* related."

A bit of tension released in his shoulders, and Beri smiled back. It was awkward that they both regarded Merlin as a father, so whenever she spoke her mind like this, it reassured him that despite his harried efforts at fitting in at school and lending his magic on the isle, things were going well between them.

"It's Gran that Mom's worried about pleasing with her cooking." Fern rolled her eyes. "You know, that thing about you never can do things right in your mother's eyes?"

Oh, aye. Lady Lark believed, as did most Windborne, that wizards should focus on nurturing the land. Beri had never understood her muttered complaints about art until Fern had turned up, and he'd learned that Lark's absent daughter, Lady Heather, was an artist. Only recently had Lady Lark seemed to accept that her daughter was *always* going to be an artist.

"I've told Gran this is your busiest season," Fern said. "No time for regular chores."

"That's why Mum will be over to set up the supper. Now, if you don't mind, I have the torch on." She swung the door.

Fern pushed back. "I need in! You're lucky the Solstice falls on a day we're off early from school, so I can finish getting the house ready, *if you aren't done yet*. The decorations are in the storage room."

She rolled her eyes. "Nice try. Go through the other door. I'm locking the interior door, so don't try it."

"Another surprise besides bread? Is it why you want me to

bring in an extra tree this year?" Fern called, but her mum closed the door in their faces.

They walked around to the back of the building, and Fern keyed in the code to the storage door. "We make most of our gifts for other people between the Solstice and Christmas. It's probably surprised her to make them beforehand. Yesterday we made our year's star together."

Before he could ask what that meant, Fern was dragging the ladder and climbing to the highest shelves. She began handing down boxes. Many boxes. By the time a dozen sat on the floor, he understood the tree decorating was a serious thing with them.

"We'll need these first." She held out a two-foot-square box labeled *Lights*. He took it, and she grabbed up another, also labeled *Lights*.

What had he gotten himself into? He gestured with his chin for her to give over the second, too. "I can carry both."

"Great. Then I can bring the special stars." Indeed, the box was labeled *Special Stars*.

Going along with Fern's plans was safer this first year, but he couldn't resist teasing. "I am verra grateful Raven and Willow are coming to share the chores you are doling out on our first day of what I was told is *vacation*."

Fern held the door for him. "That only means we can do more!" she teased back with a wink.

Aye, but having grown up with those two—Willow was a neighboring witch their age who was now prebonded with Raven—Beri knew they'd quickly get on to fun.

Inside their cabin, Fern laid her box reverently on the couch and opened the flaps. Shredded paper nested tissue-wrapped objects. She unwrapped one and held up the lacy six-pointed star of clear filaments, more spider gossamer than glass.

He whistled. "Lady Heather made that snowflake?"

"With me helping!" Fern said with what he now recognized as pretend annoyance. "And it's a star."

"Six points, a snowflake. But a spider couldn't have done better."

She laughed. "That was our inspiration." She set it back in the box and retrieved a flat box like a pie carton, which held more paper shreds. "My favorite is made of ferns—for me, obviously." Tiny, curled, glass fiddleheads bracketed each of the central fronds, and others angled into a fancy, repeating design in the middle.

"It's like a fractal," he said. "It must have taken forever."

"So long, it was the only personal piece she made us that year. We decided it had to go on the top of the tree. And it will again this year." Fern nestled the star back in its box, but couldn't fit it into the main box after her rummaging. She lifted it to the mantel stretching across the stonework behind their woodstove, but he reminded her that Lady Lark was bringing holly to decorate, so she set it on top of the stack of firewood.

"Do we nae need to build the fire once everyone gets here? For the Solstice lighting?"

"You're right." She slid the star beneath the couch. "It'll be safe there while we bring the trees in."

In the kitchen, Merlin was removing a tray of cookies from the oven and replacing it with another. He'd dressed for the celebration as he would at home—a linen shirt and leather trousers—but he'd rolled his sleeves and wore his leather apron overtop. It looked brilliantly efficient.

"Happy Solstice!" he called. "Thought I heard you, but my timing was too close." He picked up a spatula and began lifting cookie squares to a rack. "Hope you don't need me? Your Gran is worried we won't prepare things to Heather's satisfaction, so I canna burn the cookies." He glanced at the clock. "When did Heather say she'd be in?"

"Don't count on her appearing until she's called." Fern picked up a cookie. "What kind is this?"

"Traditional Scottish shortbread—"

A sharp *wheek* sounded from the floor.

They all jumped, even Beri, and he was used to the cries of Lady Lark's guinea pig.

"Hilda! Dad, what's she doing over here?"

Merlin peered around the bar at the long-haired, gray and white guinea pig. "Begging, I suppose. Lark and I have the portal open to ferry the food back and forth. I'm baking the gingerbread in her oven. Don't tell your mother."

Beri stooped and picked up the guinea pig while Fern rolled her eyes and went to the refrigerator.

"Here's some lettuce," she said, "but she's got to stay out of the sunroom. Some of my plants might be poisonous for her, and I don't want the herbs demolished."

Beri offered Hilda the lettuce, and she began eating immediately. "Hilda is just as excited as we are, but the floor is nae a safe place for her. I'll take her back to your Gran's cottage and tell her to stay."

Using the magical passageway to the isle in the cabin's bathroom, he returned the guinea pig to Hillux, swiped two cookies from Merlin and joined Fern in their jungle of a sunroom. She took the treat he gave her and ate it while she finished moving plants to clear a path for two blue spruce trees—and not small trees either. The tallest one's prickling top came level to his height.

"You are serious about this, eh?"

"Oh yeah." She grinned. "Though I admit they're getting heavy to move. Mom asked for two this year—no idea why." They bent together to push the largest pot on its rolling base. "It's been in this pot for five years. I'll probably have to break it to get it out and plant it outside."

"That is something a wee bit of magic could fix," he murmured. "You could stop it from growing."

Fern gasped in mock horror. "Poor thing. That wouldn't be fair. And Mom wouldn't like long-term magic here," she said more seriously.

Aye, it was Lady Heather's policy that nothing magical happen in her home. They both had to lift to walk the wheels over the inch-high threshold. "I—*someone* could magic it out of the pot. Then you could replace it with a smaller one, without saying anything to your mother."

Fern snorted. But after a great deal of pushing and pulling to move it—non-magically, for Orb's sake—over the living room rug, she agreed. "I'd only have to say I replaced it. She'd never think about *how* it happened."

They nearly had it to the space cleared at the window when Raven and Willow arrived through the portal. Raven wore his best trousers and leather vest and his long black hair was neatly braided, while Willow's blond hair hung loose over one of her best festival dresses. At the embroidered hem of her long skirt trotted Hilda.

"Ah, catch her," Beri called. "We canna let her in the sunroom."

Hilda dove under Heather's desk, and Willow scrambled after her, hiking up her skirt to crawl on all fours.

"Raven?" Fern called as she darted to help Willow. "Go close the sunroom door, please? And start pushing that other spruce this way!"

Raven ran off, and Beri dropped to his knees just in time to catch the chittering guinea pig when she dodged his direction.

"This floor is no place for you today, lassie." He carried her back to Hillux again. Coming back through the portal in the bathroom, he was stopped short by the tree rolling down the hall—no, *floating*.

"Ah, spells, I mean, dam—*Raven!*"

The cheeky bloke grinned. Orange-brown magic continued billowing from his hands like fog, lifting the base of the tree onto the rug.

Ach, this was far more efficient than Fern's and his struggles.

In the living room, Fern and Willow turned, and Fern's eyes widened. "Ohmigod. Stop it."

"Come off it," Raven scoffed. "Neither of you used magic for this chore?" At the girls' protests, he added, "You're idiots. She's not home."

Beri smacked his shoulder. "She can quash your magic."

"She *is* home, and she will if she sees you," Fern huffed. "It would serve you right."

"Something wrong?" Merlin called from the kitchen.

"Nay," Raven called back, then quieter, "Bunch of rotters."

Beri halfway didn't blame him. Using magic for this type of task was how they'd grown up, how they still did things at home. The first weeks visiting Colorado, he'd had a few slips, but wielding magic purposefully like this...it would thwart the trust he'd built. And Lady Heather was Raven's *mother*—what was wrong with the idiot?

He fixed Raven with a frown. "Several armloads of boxes are waiting in the workshop storage," he said. "Why don't you make yourself useful, *physically*?"

Raven scowled back, but started for the door.

Fern caught his sleeve. "Not him." She tilted her head, meeting Beri's gaze. "He can help me while you and Willow go."

Willow nodded, ever the peacemaker.

Why Fern wanted to deal with Raven was another mystery, but he'd let her take on her brother. He turned with a shrug.

Willow caught up with him at the door, and he held it for her. Their gazes met, and Willow grimaced.

"I ken," Beri muttered. "He's on the path to ruining everything."

2

GETTING THE DETAILS RIGHT

Once they'd left, Fern pointed to her brother and then the stack of CDs she'd left on top of the player. "Start the music. Low volume, please."

Raven grunted and swung around sharply enough his braid flipped, but he selected a disc. Technology fascinated him, and he'd pestered her to instruct him on their pitifully few electronics. He adjusted the volume and bass on the hammer dulcimer music she and Mom had traded for at a holiday craft show. They'd decided against anything overtly Christmasy for this first holiday together, just as they planned to keep to small handmade gifts, which was the tradition on Giuthas.

With Fern's green thumb, it'd been easy to grow lush herb pots for indoor winter picking for everyone. But for Beri... He was her first boyfriend, and this was their first holiday together. It'd taken forever to decide what to make, then several tries to get it right. She glanced toward the couch. Earlier, she hadn't wanted to put her tree topper under there because that's where she'd stashed Beri's gift before school this morning. But he'd hardly paid attention. Her gift was ready for the right moment. *I hope he likes it.*

After he got the music on, Raven poked curiously into the boxes of lights she'd dragged to an outlet. She handed him a wad of wires. "Help me test them."

"We magic the tree lit," he said as he plugged in the first. "It's simpler."

"I bet." She sighed. Her plan to involve him wasn't working. "I'm sure it's very pretty."

"If we had Solstice on the isle—"

"You know I wanted to," she said in a low voice. "Mom decided to host."

"And Merlin wouldn't go against her wishes."

Frustration flooded through her. She and Mom had planned so carefully to make this holiday perfect. "Honestly, Raven, you're not five. Get over it. There will be other years we can have it there."

He pressed his lips tight, but kept plugging in and unplugging light strands. Glad for the repetitive work that kept her from needing to say anything, Fern piled the good lights into a laundry basket and kept handing him the next from the box. Two strings didn't work so she dropped them behind the couch and retrieved two boxes of new ones from a bag there. "These are enough for the tree outside."

"You'll repair the others later?"

"Well…" She hated to admit this. "It's hard to find the burned-out bulbs or broken wires. We usually just get new. It's a waste, I know."

He snorted and retrieved a wad of the faulty lights. Fingers aglow with magic, Raven unrolled it while feeling along the wires. The strand began lighting without electricity.

Fern gasped and immediately felt foolish. *Of course he can do this.* "You better not let Mom see."

He chuckled. "I notice you're not yelling, 'Stop it,' this time."

He was so exasperating, but after weeks of arguing, she was taking a cue from Beri and ignoring most of Raven's comments.

At a spot that didn't light, he pinched either side of a chew in the plastic. The wires slunk out like worms and welded to each other. The lights lit. He twitched the cord, and the plastic flowed over the repair, creating a lump. "I assume it doesn't need to be a pretty fix?"

"Uh, no. Thanks." She retrieved the other strand and traded him. He worked along this one, and it seemed safe to bring up his earlier complaint. "Sorry you're upset we aren't celebrating at Dad's. I'll support doing that next year, and Mom should agree."

Raven glanced at her before returning to his study of this strand. "It's not that so much. We can still magic the lights at home and invite the birds into the greenery. They like it a lot. We hide seeds for them, so it's like a game." He drew a breath. "This year…it's a reminder of other Solstices growing up when I wondered why my mum left. I know why now, that it wasn't my fault, but…" He shrugged.

Fern bit her lip. Their mom's reasons for leaving Giuthas had been incredible.

"There's still a part of me that is a bit angry that I missed…stuff."

She knew just what he meant. "Having both your mom and dad there, like other kids."

He looked at the ceiling. "Don't tell Beri, because after he came to live with us, it made me feel like a selfish git when he'd lost both his parents."

"I won't, if you don't tell him I've always thought the same, about missing stuff." Their gazes met, nearly as if looking in a mirror, save for his hazel eyes not matching her brown ones. Raven smiled the same twisted smile she knew she was giving him. They broke out laughing at the same time. She flung an arm around him and gave him a quick hug.

"Total truth time," she said. "It's been just Mom and me for forever, so having all of you here, when you do things your way and we do things ours…it's hard."

The front door opened, letting in a gust of cold air along with Willow and Beri. Fern tilted her head to Raven's. "Please give us a chance? Mom and I both really want this to go well for everyone."

He nodded. "I will give it my best go."

"Thanks." Fern grinned for real. "She made soup and, instead of buying bread, has actually made it homemade."

Raven's brows lifted, followed by his nose. He sniffed. "I don't smell bread."

Willow set her boxes down and nudged him. "You will when you go to the studio to fetch the rest of these boxes."

Raven eyed her, then took her hand and led the way outside. Meeting Beri's gaze, Fern waved for them to follow in time to witness Raven testing the scent at the edge of the off-limits studio door. After everything was stacked in the cabin's hallway, Fern picked up the laundry basket of lights.

"Let's get the outdoor tree strung first."

Outside, Beri checked the mountaintops as he and Raven carried the ladders from the shed. The clouds had definitely thickened during the time they'd been inside. A stronger scent of ponderosa pine drifted on the air—so that must mean moisture was moving in. But nary a flake fell while they climbed up next to a blue spruce and began winding lights around its top. He complained about the lack of snow to Fern as she handed them another light string.

She laughed. "Tell you what? We'll wait to take the lights down during a snowfall."

"At least you got to be here during the last," Raven grumbled to Beri. "We have this easy por—"

"Ah-ah." Beri shook a finger at him around the treetop.

Raven groaned as he took the string of lights. "Easy travel," he corrected, "and we still aren't seeing snow."

"You feel put out?" Beri huffed. "I had to spend eight hours of the one snow day inside a school building and two more inside a bus. I had only the walk home and a few snowballs pitched at Fern."

"Did you hit her?"

Beri wagged his brows. "Aye, but she got me back far better. Beware of the lass when she becomes good enough to throw—" *Shockballs*, he was going to say. A slip like that and Lady Heather would ground him, even if the word had no real meaning to humans. "The point is, after a restricted day, homework and hours working on the isle, the snow was gone."

"No sympathy." Raven grinned. "I am equally busy with *you* gone."

"Glad to see you in better humor. Did Fern set you straight?"

"You might say that, but Willow also thanked me quite thoroughly for my Solstice gift."

He'd noticed Willow was wearing the wooden bracelets Raven had carved of three different colors of wood. They'd gotten the idea when they'd jointly made their gifts for everyone else.

"I must say I'm a little surprised. They aren't useful at all, only decorative."

"Mate, you need to learn to read the lasses. They like girlie things, or at least Willow does." He took the lights and worked them into the branches on his side. "Don't worry, Fern will like what you made her, because it's the first gift you've given her. Then you have a whole year more to figure out what she likes." Raven passed him the lights.

Beri took the balled string and stepped down a rung on the

ladder. Following much consideration, he *had* used Raven's example and made something girlie for Fern. But Fern wasn't like Willow, who wore dresses and prettied up her hair. Fern was in jeans and a fleece now and had said nothing to him about changing from school clothes for their celebration. "A study of Fern's preferences must wait until after I finish up this schooling. Its treadmill leaves me blasted little free time."

"What's a treadmill?" Raven asked.

"Geez, the things you don't know!" Fern climbed up even with their knees and handed Raven another strand. "Thank goodness no one is around to hear you ask about common machinery, but we need to get you back in the house as fast as possible."

"I could finish faster, if you—"

"Don't even think it," Fern said, but she was smiling. That faded quickly. "Bad news for you, Beri." She pointed upward. "The sky is clearing. It'll be stars tonight, not snow."

Once the last lights were on the outside tree, Fern connected the final strand to the extension cord. "Okay, all set here."

Willow frowned at Raven. "But they aren't alight. I thought you fixed them?"

He lifted his hands. "My work is good. Check it yourself."

"I have this outlet turned off from inside the house," Fern said. She walked a few steps toward the cabin, then hesitated. "Usually, we light them when we light the fire, but Mom and I agreed we shouldn't totally do things our way. Could we at least wait until she and Dad and Gran are here to see it light up the first time?"

Willow touched her arm. "You have a Yule lighting, too?"

"I guess?" It'd taken Fern a moment to recognize the word she'd always rhymed with *mule*. Willow pronounced it *Yull*, in her Giuthas accent. "We clean the grate in the woodstove and lay a new fire. We light it first, then the trees, and eat supper as we decorate. Most people around here celebrate Yule by eating a rolled cake that's decorated to look like a log. But I've caught on that it's not a celebration of food."

Willow nodded. "The Yule lighting symbolizes the turning of the Solstice and the return of additional daylight. We don't mind waiting to do the tree lighting as part of it. You have your starter?"

The way Willow phrased it didn't sound like she meant matches.

Raven lifted a ladder. "Dad has taken care of that."

"So has Lady Lark," Beri said with a laugh. "I'm nae sure their little woodstove will hold it all." He hefted the second ladder onto his shoulder and followed Raven.

Fern grabbed up the basket. She and Willow fell into step. "What are you talking about?"

"We save a piece of burnt wood from the prior year's Yule fire to start the next year's log. The tradition connects the years like the renewal of life."

"We don't do that—well, we haven't before, but we could start."

Willow wrinkled her nose. "It does nae sound too superstitious to you?"

Fern laughed and linked arms with her. "It's just tradition, right? Not, um—hold on a second." They entered the house and closed the door, but still Fern dropped her voice to ask, "No spells involved?"

Willow stiffened, her brow furrowed. "In our family, someone is given the honor of lighting the Yule with..." She tapped her pointer finger with her thumb. "Magic. But no spells lie in the Yule wood."

They took off their jackets and hung them in the quiet hallway. The CD had ended. Dad's deep voice drifted from the kitchen. The cabin smelled spicy—like gingerbread—so Gran must have come over with Dad's cake. Fern's mouth began to water. Now that most everything was ready and Raven's grumpiness was put away, she could think about setting out the supper things in the living rom.

But Willow was still frowning. "Is something wrong?" Fern asked. "Around here, this is supposed to be a happy time."

She wrung her hands. "I really hadn't considered that you and Lady Heather kept human traditions in this world when we created your gifts. But if I change things, the boys will be upset."

"Then...our gifts are magicked?"

Willow nodded.

"If it's something you made me, of course I'll like it. Why are we worried about the boys?"

"Ach." Willow bit her lip. "We didn't tell you, because..."

Fern took a hairbrush from a drawer in the hall table. She smoothed her tangled hair while waiting for Willow to decide if she wanted to spill this. Willow's blond hair still hung perfectly. Magic. Willow did all sorts of things without even thinking of them, but she still worried about what everyone thought, the same as Fern did. She glanced toward the couch again. *Argh, I can hardly stand waiting to see what Beri thinks!*

"The three of us made our gifts together," Willow said. "We have for years. Everyone has liked them, so if I change things for you, they'll be upset, but Lady Heather may be angry if I don't."

Beri made my gift with them? That seemed...odd. And disappointing. *Geez, Fern, don't be selfish.* If that was the way they did things...well, she liked Beri too much for stuff to get in the way.

Fern dropped the brush back, then grasped Willow's shoulders. "Listen, my vote is you give them to us as they are. Maybe we can't leave them out for other people to see. Maybe we have to keep them over at Gran's. But you have made something because you care for us, and that's what gifts are about."

Willow's brow was still creased, but she nodded and hugged Fern.

"I forgot to ask how your family's celebration was," Fern said. "Did you have a good time?" The Forest family would have already had their celebration, since the isle was seven hours ahead of Colorado.

"Oh, aye." She smiled. "It's so exciting for the little ones, so much noisier than your house. I'm glad to be invited, but it'll be hard to convince Lady Lark that I'm not hungry after our feast. Oh." Her hand flew to her mouth. "*And* your mother. Please help me distract her?"

Fern pulled Willow into the living room and gestured to the trees standing in the middle of the room. "With decorating, we'll have so much going on that no one will notice if you eat or not."

Holly branches now graced the end tables and the center of the mantel. Below, two pieces of charred wood sat on the hearth's floor slates—the promised Yule starters.

In her pocket, Fern's phone buzzed, and she checked it.

Mom's text read: *The bread is done, and I'm finished as well. Could you tell your dad, and send help to carry things in?*

"Oh no!" She showed Willow the message. "I don't have the lights on the indoor trees."

Willow went to tell Dad, and Fern got the second box of tested lights and started on one of the trees still in the middle of the rug. The boys came in. Raven and Willow left to help Mom, and Beri began stringing the second tree a few feet away.

"Thanks," Fern said as they circled and tucked lights between the boughs. "Did I tell you that yet?"

"Maybe." He chuckled. "We've been a wee bit busy with your chores today."

"And you wanted to sleep on your vacation. Sorry."

"And spend time with you, you ken?" They were squeezing past each other between the trees, and he caught her around the waist. "Like this. Did you notice Lady Lark has fully decorated?" He pointed upward.

Sprigs of mistletoe tied with a red ribbon hung from a log beam.

Fern burst out laughing. "You put her up to that."

His green eyes sparkling, Beri tugged her close, his arms warm around her. "I did nae," he whispered. "But I'm nae about to let it go to waste."

He leaned in, and so did she, even though Mom—or Dad or Gran!—could walk in at any moment. Yet Beri's curly hair and freckle-dusted cheeks were so tempting. And his lips! Knowing how great they'd taste, she licked hers and closed her eyes.

His lips brushed hers. A buzz tingled over her skin, a warning of rising magic.

Nooo! Her eyes flashed open, and she froze. Beri's gaze met hers, his eyes greener than seconds ago. *Hold on a second—*

"My magic is still locked in my cores," she whispered. "From being at school. This is you."

"Me? Blast." He flinched back—into the tree. It swayed, and he jerked sideways to avoid it.

Laughing, she caught handfuls of his sweater, and they lurched upright together. "I don't think the gift I made you is going to get the same reaction, so maybe I should wish you Happy Solstice now."

He grinned, his face inches from hers. "You have made me something? I made something just for you."

He had? Her heart soared. "Oh yeah? That's cool."

"And expected on the Solstice," Raven said. "Just as kissing is."

They stumbled apart, Fern feeling heat rising over her cheeks. "I didn't hear you come in," she mumbled, which only made Raven grin broader.

"Nay, you wouldn't have. Better me than Mom."

Willow elbowed him. "Don't tease them."

"But it's so blasted easy." He set a large wrapped package on the couch, and Willow added a basket of smaller wrapped gifts.

Mom was giving something large? They'd discussed that small things were given on Giuthas, and it wasn't like Mom to favor one person with a large piece of glasswork. Unless... "Is that for Dad?"

The front door opened, letting in a welcome cool gust—*how could I have missed the chill before?*—and her mother.

Mom carried a bundled dishtowel that had to contain the bread, because the doughy freshness of it wafted across the room. She'd changed into her favorite floor-length dress for the holidays, one patterned with holly leaves and bright dots of red berries. Her curly hair now hung loose.

Footsteps thudded from the kitchen, and Gran emerged, also in a green linen dress and with her hair looking just like Mom's. She carried a bowl of salad, and Dad followed, bearing the Crock-Pot. He'd taken off his apron and put on his leather vest.

"The rest is ready to bring in," he said. "Could everyone lend a hand—oh. Are the trees partaking, too?" The spruce trees still stood in the middle of the room.

"Just a sec!" *So much for changing into a dress.* Fern retrieved her lights and began looping them over the branches. While she and Beri finished up, the others tracked back and forth from the kitchen, setting the coffee table with food and dishes. In minutes, they'd moved the trees to the windows and plugged them in, but didn't throw the switch. With the whole family, ornament boxes, presents and the trees, their small living room was crowded. She should get her gifts from the sunroom, though the herb pots weren't wrapped, just decorated with bows...

She stepped that way when Dad said, "We could expand the space a mite if we pushed the couch against your desk, Heather. Would that be all right?"

"Hold it!" Fern spun back and threw up her hands before

Mom could answer. "I've got something under there." Heart racing at the close call—one wrong push would have broken them!—she fell to her knees at the couch. Her fingers scraped the bare floor under it. She reached to swipe deeper—and hit nothing.

"Geez," she muttered. She stretched out on her belly and peered under.

Her special star—and the gift for Beri—were gone.

3

WHAT'S IMPORTANT?

Beri crossed to the end of the couch opposite from where Fern now searched under the coffee table, then under the couch again. Her gaze met his. *She's more upset than she's letting on.*

"Ready to move it?" Merlin asked.

Beri waved to signal no at the same time Fern blurted, "No, don't...I mean, I have to find something first. I don't want it crushed."

Everyone else looked confused. Beri knelt beside her. "You need some help?"

"Well..." Fern pressed her fingers to her temples. "Did you move my star, by chance?"

He shook his head. "Where could it have gone?"

"I don't know." She looked up at Lady Heather. "Did you... you haven't been in the house all afternoon." She glanced around at the others. "Did anyone move a box with shredded paper this big"—she shaped the size of the pie box with her hands—"and another wrapped gift slightly smaller, but also flat?" She glanced at him when she said this.

Ach, the gift for me.

"Oh," Lady Heather said. "Which star?"

Fern swallowed. "The treetop one. After I showed it to Beri, I thought it'd be safer under here with my other gift. I didn't want to stuff everything back into the storage box."

Lady Heather nodded thoughtfully, and Fern added, "Sorry."

"We'll find it. Perhaps in your excitement you only thought about putting it there, but decided on another spot."

Fern's mother wove behind the couch and lifted the files and papers on her desk to search, but Beri remembered clearly that Fern put the star box under the couch after deciding it'd be too vulnerable on top of the firewood.

Still…he should be encouraging. "We've been moving lots of things in today." He gave Fern's shoulders a quick squeeze. "We'll all look and find it."

"Just a plain star?" Raven asked.

Fern glared at him.

"I mean, it's not magical?"

Fern blew out her breath. "Oh, no, not magical."

"I am trying to help," Raven said indignantly. "So the most likely place is still on the floor?"

"I guess?"

They all searched under the furniture, in the corners, through Lady Heather's business files under her desk and around the ornament boxes stacked in the hall. Lady Heather even went through the box that held all the other stars.

Finally, Fern slumped against the couch, and Beri dropped to the floor next to her.

"'Twas your gift to me, right?" he whispered, and she nodded glumly. "I can tell it's upset you to lose it, but I do nae mind getting it late. We should let folks get on with eating."

"I know." She rubbed her forehead. "Okay, thanks, everyone, but I don't want to hold up supper and our Solstice celebration any longer."

At Lady Heather's nod, Merlin opened the woodstove and

began building the fire. Lady Lark started ladling out bowls of steaming soup that Willow placed spoons in and set out. Raven cut the bread and slathered the slices with butter.

Fern leaned her head back on the couch and looked over at Beri. "I can't believe I lost my tree star. We'll be starless, just like you're snowless."

"Oh, starless night," he sang softly, mimicking a song he'd heard from Fern's music. But that didn't get her to smile. He stroked his thumb over the back of her hand. "It could nae have left the house."

Holding the large, wrapped gift, Lady Heather squatted before Fern. "Perhaps this is the year to place a different star on the top of the tree."

Fern peered at her. "Is that why you wanted two trees this year? And what's in that box?"

Lady Heather smiled. "Maybe."

"Mom? Who is that for?"

"Raven."

Fern met Raven's gaze as he turned from the coffee table.

"Me?" he asked.

Mom leaned to whisper in Fern's ear. "I hope you don't mind, Meadowsweet. I didn't expect you to lose your star, but…I want to do this for him." She traced a pattern on Fern's forehead and kissed it. The magic in the ward spread with a warm tingle. When Mom lifted her head, her eyes were teary.

Oh man, this was likely some compensation for the guilt Mom felt for missing Raven growing up.

Mom rose and gave a forehead kiss and ward to Raven, while he stood dumbfounded with a slice of bread in one hand and the butter knife in the other.

That got Fern smiling. *Okay, missing only a few items isn't going to spoil my first Solstice with all my family finally here.*

Then, all sentiment seemingly aside, Mom took the bread and knife, passed them to Gran, handed Raven a napkin and ordered him to wipe his hands.

"But," he sputtered as he did, "we haven't lit the Yule log yet. Presents aren't allowed until after the lighting!"

Dad straightened from the woodstove and exchanged looks with Mom. She rolled her eyes, and he gave a shrug that Fern knew had come to mean he would agree with her decision. Dad nearly always agreed. He wanted their family to stay together.

"Ye have trained your boys quite well," Mom said. "Can we not make an exception for the one at the top of this box? It's long overdue."

Dad nodded, and Raven took the box from Mom.

He dropped into a chair and tore off the wrapping paper. The cardboard carton beneath was the same type they used for all Mom's glasswork. In fact, as Raven unsealed the flaps, Fern knew what he was opening. She tugged at Beri's hand, and they got up off the floor to see better.

Inside, shredded paper filled the corners as it did in all their ornament boxes and on top sat a ten-inch-square lidded box. Raven glanced up at Mom.

"That's the one to open now," she said.

He worked off the lid and carefully raked back the shreds. From them, he lifted a clear glass star that, like Fern's, had also been designed as a tree topper. However, instead of ferns, perched birds flanked the six arms, and in the center, a bird in flight burst forth.

"Ravens," he said softly.

"When did you make it?" Fern asked Mom.

"When we created yours," she said, and it sounded half like an apology. "I also created an ornament for Raven each year. I had to." Her hands clutched the folds of her skirt, and she pressed her lips together.

Oh no! Mom was on her very edge—nervous about if Raven liked the star on top of what he thought about her saving up gifts for him all these years. *That's why she apologized to me already. She's worried I might be jealous.*

Fern slipped her hand into Mom's and squeezed. "It's great, Mom," she whispered.

"Are you saying there are sixteen more in this box?" Raven asked, and Mom nodded. Carefully, he handed the star to Willow and set the box aside. Then he rose and hugged Mom a very long time.

Gran sniffed. "Is tha' nae the most lovely thing?"

Mom turned with a delighted smile. "Why, thank you, Mum."

Fern suppressed a smile. This *was* quite the compliment from Gran.

Dad hugged Mom, too, and whispered something to her that made her smile more, so everything was good. After everyone had a chance to admire the star's detail, Raven laid it back in the box.

"Hey," Fern said. "What are you doing? That goes on the top of the tree." She pointed and nudged him toward the tallest spruce.

"I assume without magic?" he asked, and when she showed him how to do it, he wired it on over the cluster of three lights she'd fastened to the tree's leader.

They admired it all over again—and rightly so. It was one of Mom's best, and Fern was excited for Raven. "It's a light splitter," she told him. "You're in for a treat when we turn on the lights."

Dad gestured to the woodstove. "The fire is ready for the lighting. Are we all ready?"

Mom turned out the overhead lights, and Raven ran to turn off the others in the kitchen. With the house darkened, the view through the windows showed the spruce and pines surrounding the cabin. Everybody clustered into a semicircle facing the hearth.

"Heather?" Dad asked quietly. "Who shall do the lighting this year?"

"I'd like Mum to have the honor, if she will?"

Gran swished her hand. "Because I am the oldest here?" she grumbled.

Mom laughed. "Of course. We need to pick up the old traditions, and what better way to do it than to grant this down through our ages?" She handed Gran the box of matches.

Gran shook her head as she accepted them, but Fern could tell she was pleased. "Not our tradition, but it'll do." She struck one and held it to the dried pine needles and sticks Dad had stacked against the charred logs he and Gran had brought. Soon, flames licked across everything.

Beri slipped an arm around Fern's waist, warm and comforting, as they watched the growing light. *It'll be all right that I don't have a special gift for him. He wanted time together, and we have that.*

Gran poked the fire. "I believe it's time to add this year's Yule log. Did you select a particular one, Heather?"

"Any of the cedars I propped to the side. They give off a nice fragrance."

Dad leaned over the pile on the hearth and picked up the smallest of the round logs. His back gave an odd squeak as he rose, and he froze, holding the log.

"Dad?" Fern clutched his arm. "You okay?"

He started laughing. "Aye, I'm nae that old, lass."

"Nooo." Mom groaned. "Don't tell me we have mice again!"

"Ye don't, but I think this is something Fern needs to address." He beckoned her to take his place.

She searched where he pointed, trying to make out what was in the shadows of the logs. Two bulging eyes glinted back at her. "Hilda!"

"Hilda?" Everyone repeated the guinea pig's name in either surprise or laughter.

"Careful picking her up," Dad said. "I think she has something of yours."

"Ohmigod, she made a bed of my star box!" Fern fell to her knees.

Beri leaned over her. "Ach. If it's not broken, I'll be surprised." He spread his fingers and flushed green magic into the enclosed space.

Eek—he was using magic outside of the isle. Fern crossed her fingers that Mom wouldn't get mad.

The guinea pig rose, suspended in a magical hammock and squealing her irritation. He scooped his large hands under her, and when he had her, the magic winked out. Hilda turned in his hands, trying to escape, but he clucked to quiet her against his chest, casting a guilty glance over his shoulder. "Sorry, Lady Heather."

"I didn't see a thing," Mom said. "Not on the Solstice."

Raven crowded in. "How under the Orb did she get it back there?" He lit his own fingers to study the cramped space.

Now able to see, Fern carefully lifted the box. "I think she ate half the paper."

"Probably why she slept so soundly," Gran muttered.

Her glass star was visible on a sparse bedding of shredded paper instead of nesting into it. Fern picked it up by one of its arms and held it aloft, turning it to and fro. Was it…? "It has all the points—oh." One of the ferns was gone.

"I can fix it," Mom said, taking the box and picking out the broken fern. "Easier than the structural parts." She set it on her desk.

Willow replaced her and tapped Fern's shoulder. "Is your other package there, too?"

Was it? Raven had cut off his energy, and Mom hadn't yelled at him, so Fern lit her fingers and reached under the logs. Wedged in the back was her gift for Beri.

She scrambled up and touched a finger to Hilda's nose. "You sneak!" She handed her gift to Beri. "It might be broken, too, but Happy Solstice!"

Beri kissed her forehead, making Hilda *wheek* and everyone else laugh. "But I canna find out until we've finished the lighting." He looked at Gran.

"Merlin?" she said. "Pass me the log."

The flames had died back, but with more tinder and Gran's stoking—and maybe magic?—last year's logs lit again. The new log caught, sending its cedar scent through the room.

Fern attached her star to the top of the other tree and stepped back. "We're ready to light. Raven?" She pivoted and clasped his elbow. "You should do the honors for this lighting." She led him to the switch. "But watch while you do!"

Raven flipped the switch. Specks of light sprang to life over the trees, and the top—wow. The raven star sent rays of light in all directions, and their first-time Solstice guests gasped.

Fern met Mom's gaze and gave her a thumbs-up. Showing off the rest of their stars was gonna be fun. "Watch outside now!" She darted to the switch in the hall for the outdoor outlets, flicked it and grinned as everyone *aahed*—and Beri whooped.

As she came back in, he wrapped his arm around her waist. She snuggled against his side—tingly with excited magic—as they stood together gazing at the lit trees brightening the dusky woodlands.

"'Tis beautiful," he whispered. "I ken now why you've been so bubbly today. The glass and lights are a lovely way to create magic in the human world."

She rested her head on his shoulder. The tree lights sparkled through the needles as the wind shifted the branches. The only thing missing was—

"Ach, is that… Aye, it's snowing!"

Fern laughed. "No way. I see clear skies over the treetops."

But it was.

They threw open the door and spilled into the yard. Giant snowflakes pelted down from a clear star-filled sky, catching in everyone's hair, filling the needles along the spruce branches and burying the lightbulbs so they glowed.

"How can this be?" Merlin said in wonder.

Mom turned him around to where a bank of clouds hugged the distant mountain ridge. "'Tis a storm in the west. See how big they are? These flakes have fluttered quite a distance, growing as they did, before their weight brought them down."

Dad smiled. "You mean it was magic."

With a frown, Mom opened her mouth, and Dad kissed her.

Beside Fern, Beri chuckled. "I will nae argue that, since snow is what I wished for."

He was still carrying her gift—though, thankfully, not Hilda. "Open your present," she told him.

He ripped the paper off the box—which didn't look crushed —and opened it. Whistling, he lifted the glass piece she'd made him, a flameworked snowflake with her best filigree swirls and toothpick-thin snowflakes filling the spaces between each of the arms.

Her breath whooshed out. "It actually survived a chubby guinea pig dragging it around and sleeping on it!"

"Aye," he said breathlessly. "'Tis beautiful, Fern. A snowflake I can admire all year long."

Then, holding it aloft, he hooked an arm around her shoulders and pulled her in for a kiss. Heart beating like the little drummer boy's drum, she kissed him back.

Raven hooted from across the yard, but it was Mom's voice becoming louder as she obviously walked closer that made

Fern pull back. Her excited giggling filled the inches between them.

Beri whispered, "Thank you. Here." He pushed a small package into her hand. "I-I hope you like it."

She stopped halfway through tearing off the paper. "Were you as nervous as I was about giving each other gifts?"

His face scrunched so tight his freckles looked ready to pop. "Would you just open it so my stomach will settle before we eat?"

Tossing him a grin, she pulled at the paper, and a round medallion on a long cord fell into her hand. "I can't see it," she complained.

He pointed a finger, then groaned and dragged her to the lit spruce and pulled a bunch of lights toward her. The medallion was wooden, two layers, light wood over dark, and carved into it was a delicate little scene of a rabbit, a toad and a bird hiding between blades of grass with flowers nodding overhead and butterflies flitting above.

"Awwww," she squealed and threw her arms around him. "It's wonderful!"

"I thought you might like to carry the Meadows with you here, but then I worried it might remind you too much of work or not being able to get to the projects you have planned. I wondered if you'd wear jewelry—"

She pressed her lips to his. He stopped talking and blinked. Then, when she parted from him, he clutched handfuls of her fleece and pulled her to him again, his lips warm and spicy-tasting against hers. She leaned into him, snow pricking their faces and melting. When he raised his head, she said, "I love it!" and lifted up on tiptoes to keep recklessly kissing—until a badly packed snowball hit her shoulder and splattered their cheeks.

Beri grinned at her. "Brilliant. I'm glad to hear that and wish to spend more time thanking you properly, but Raven has unknowingly requested a lesson in snowball throwing that I believe that we both should give him."

***

Hours later, Fern snuggled next to the others on the couch with only the dying fire and glinting ornaments for light. Beri had fallen asleep within five minutes of Gran and Fern's parents heading to bed, and Raven, at the other end of the couch, not long after. She and Willow had whispered in the middle before Willow had drooped onto Raven's shoulder.

Fern's own head rested on Beri's arm, still around her. Everything had been a success. Mom's soup and bread, Dad's cookies and Gran's salad dressed with herbal vinegar. That had been Gran's gift—bottles in different herb combinations from her garden. They'd laughed that Fern also gifted plants. Dad gave everyone bags of honey candy drops made from his hives, and Mom presented each new family member with a Colorado favorite—glass columbine flowers.

As Willow had told her, she, Raven and Beri had collaborated on round wooden trinket boxes. Fern and her mom had seen similar crafts at art shows, so this certainly fit into the human world. But then Willow instructed them to run their thumbs around the lid decoration, lighter wood carved into a crescent moon.

Fern pulled hers out of her fleece pocket and rubbed the edge. As her thumb completed the circumference, a glow rose. Mom had been impressed and complimented both the craftsmanship and spellwork.

Beri shifted at her back. "Do you like it?" he whispered.

"Very much. Mom did, too. I think she'll let us keep them here."

"So, it was a good Solstice?"

She rolled over and laid her head on his chest. "The best."

He yawned. "Aye. Snow *and* stars. Gifts, good food, togetherness. But..."

"What?"

"It needs more sleeping hours, you ken?"

Fern rapped him, which earned her a chuckle and Beri's arm tightening around her. She brought her meadow medallion into the glow of the box's moon for a last look, then turned it off. "Happy Solstice," she whispered.

"Verra much so," he murmured.

THANK YOU

*Along with my Windborne friends, I wish you and yours a warm and safe
holiday season!*
Laurel

ABOUT THE AUTHOR

Before kids, Laurel Wanrow studied and worked as a naturalist —someone who leads wildflower walks and answers calls about the snake that wandered into your garage. During a stint of homeschooling, she turned her writing skills to fiction to share her love of the land, magical characters and fantastical settings.

She's the author of *The Luminated Threads* series, a Victorian historical fantasy mixing witches, shapeshifters and a sweet romance in a secret corner of England, and *The Windborne*, a nature-focused YA fantasy series set in our world.

When not living in her fantasy worlds, Laurel camps, hunts fossils, and argues with her husband and two new adult kids over whose turn it is to clean house. Though they live on the East Coast, a cherished family cabin in the Colorado Rockies holds Laurel's heart.

Visit her website at www.laurelwanrow.com.

facebook.com/laurelwanrowauthor

twitter.com/laurelwanrow

instagram.com/laurelwanrowauthor

bookbub.com/authors/laurel-wanrow

pinterest.com/laurelwanrow